Lay-ups and Long Shots

An anthology of short stories by

Joseph Bruchac

Lynea Bowdish

David Lubar

Terry Trueman

CS Perryess

Dorian Cirrone

Jamie McEwan

Max Elliot Anderson

Peggy Duffy

DARBY CREEK PUBLISHING

Cataloging-in-Publication

Lay-ups and long shots : an anthology of short stories / by Joseph Bruchac ... [et al.].
     p. ; cm.
ISBN 978-1-58196-078-5
Ages 10 and up.—Summary: A collection of nine short stories about middle-schoolers and sports. They range from basketball, to running, Ping-Pong, dirt biking, surfing, kayaking, place kicking, soccer, and. a game of "H-O-R-S-E"
1. Sports—Juvenile fiction. 2. Athletic ability—Juvenile fiction. 3. Sportsmanship—Juvenile fiction. [1. Sports—Fiction. 2. Athletic ability—Fiction. 3. Sportsmanship—Fiction.] I. Title. II. Author.
PS648.S78 L39 2008
813/.0108357 dc22
OCLC: 209781485

Published by Darby Creek Publishing
7858 Industrial Parkway
Plain City, OH 43064
www.darbycreekpublishing.com

Printed in the United States of America

2 4 6 8 10 9 7 5 3 1

CONTENTS

☆ *Joseph Bruchac* ☆

Joseph Bruchac is a prolific writer and storyteller whose work often reflects his Abenaki Indian heritage and his rural upbringing in the Adirondack mountain foothills. Most of his childhood, he was always the kid picked last or left out when it came to sports—until he grew six inches between his junior and senior years in high school and went on to play football, become a champion heavyweight wrestler, and throw the shotput and discus in track. His books about sports include *Native American Games and Stories* (coauthored with his son, James), *The Warriors*, and *The Way*.

SWISH: A Basketball Story

by

Joseph Bruchac

"What's the difference between a fourth string basketball player and a masochist?"

It was my second day of trying to become a high school basketball player. Thus it was my responsibility to reply to that question asked by Kelly Donahue, the team captain and leading scorer. And just in case I didn't realize that was my role, I got elbowed in the ribs by him as he asked it.

"I don't know," I sighed. "What?"

"A masochist knows when to stop punishing himself."

If there's one joke to sum up my attempted career in basketball, I guess that's it. Even suggesting I might be a fourth stringer was a compliment.

I'd practiced some at home next to the general store and gas station where I lived with my grandparents. I'd gotten a new basketball from them for Christmas. As soon as the snow cleared, Grampa Jesse had nailed up a bent basketball hoop with a torn net to the shingled side of the building as close to regulation height as the low roof allowed. There we played intermittant games of HORSE through the summer and fall—broken up by the arrival of customers when Grampa would stow the ball behind the door while he pumped gas. Since we lived way out in the country, there usually weren't other kids of my age to play with.

But even though I usually won against my seventy-year-old grandfather, I couldn't seem to improve.

Maybe it was also due to the peculiarity of that makeshift basketball court that had been set up for me. Their store on the corner of Route 9N and Middle Grove Road was called the Splinterville Hill Filling Station for good reason. It was halfway up a steep hill once paved with splintery planks. Our driveway, on the Middle Grove Road side of the store, had an outside slant toward 9N, the busy state road that my nervous grandmother always urged me away from. (Though I was fourteen I still wasn't allowed to ride my bike there.) On 9N, a steady stream of cars and big trucks rumbled by. Even going uphill they traveled at a rapid clip because, as my grandmother put it, they had to "get up a head of steam" to make it to the top.

I wasn't allowed to play alone. Grampa had to be there to make sure the ball didn't get away from me and go bouncing into traffic. The surface of my so-called ball court was only half paved, the old blacktop rippled with frost. A bounce might come back to your hand or careen off toward parts unknown. All I could realistically practice was shooting from ten or twenty feet out. No dribbling or passing or even lay-ups. However, I'd developed a few special shots in our HORSE contests, where you had to match the shot of the person ahead of you or earn a letter, with the first person getting all five being the loser. For example, I could sometimes make a tricky basket by throwing the ball down so hard on a certain flat piece of blacktop that it would bounce up high and go in. Not something you could do in a real game.

By my second day of trying out for the team I'd discovered that there were only three things I'd excelled at during practice. The first was traveling. The second was double-dribbling. And if you don't know what those two no-nos are, then you know less about the game than I did when I was an undersized teenager at Saratoga High School.

And what was the third thing? I had a natural ability for fouling. Small as I was, when I went for the ball, I was almost always able to get it—along with a loud blast from the whistle because I'd knocked somebody down or accidentally popped somebody in the nose with my elbow and slapped their hands taking the ball away. To make matters worse, my first reaction whenever that happened was to complain.

"I didn't foul. I know I didn't. Maybe somebody else tripped you. I didn't do that, did I? I'm sure I just hit the ball and not your arm. Honest."

Coach Dalrymple called me over to him. "Bruchac," he said, "what are you, a basketball player or bowling ball? No, I don't want you to answer that. Just take a seat."

Why did I want to play a game for which I had no natural ability? I guess there's only one word to explain it. *Swish!* That's the sound a ball makes when you shoot it from ten or twenty or even thirty feet away and it arcs up—a hook or a two-handed foul shot or a one handed fall-away jumper, it doesn't matter—and falls right through without touching the rim. *Swish!* The sweet sound it makes as it ripples through the net.

I'd done that. Swished the ball. It was almost always when I was alone in the gym or shooting with Grampa at the old nailed-up hoop. And I only managed it about one shot out of a hundred. Never twice in a row. But when it happened, it was like an electrical current shot through me from the top of my head on down to my toes. *Swish!* Pure magic. My fondest hopes in basketball were first to hear that *swish*, and second to play a real basketball game on a real court with Grampa watching and telling people proudly, "That's my grandson." Making him proud of me was as important as anything.

So I tried to stick with it, even though on the second day after practice when I came back to my locker I found my shoes with no laces and my street clothes tied together in knots. And on the third day, I got tripped by somebody—it might have been Pat Harley, who I'd accidentally elbowed in the nose—so that I ended up falling over a bench, cracking the left lens of my glasses and skinning my knee. I don't think the other players meant to be cruel. I was just the obvious target for the instinctive response of adolescent jocks confronted by absolute incompetence in their chosen field. You couldn't criticize them for their behavior any more than you'd fault a pride of lions for pulling down a wounded wildebeest.

Being hopelessly inept at such small details as passing, catching the ball, dribbling, and shooting also got me noticed by the coaches. Not only was I creating havoc whenever I was allowed on the floor, they saw something that I didn't. If I kept on bumping into, tripping, and elbowing the other players—even in drills—the next time I ventured into the locker room after practice with eighteen larger, resentful fellow players, I might not come out alive.

Partway through my fourth day, Coach Dalyrymple walked out on the court, took the ball from my hand, and tossed it to another player. He put one arm around my shoulder and led me over to the stands by the back door to the gym.

"Bruchac," he said in a soft voice, "I know your grandparents. I know you're a good kid. But this game's not for you. Maybe next year if you get six inches taller. Hit the showers."

"But practice isn't over yet," I protested.

"It's over for you, son," Coach Dalyrymple squeezed my shoulder as I lifted one hand to push my glasses—which now had two cracked lenses—back up my nose. He spoke slowly, to make sure I understood. And though the tone of his voice was kind, those words hurt. "You are not going to be on the basketball team. Go home."

When I got off the late bus that afternoon, my grandparents weren't home. The store was locked and there was a note from Grama on the house door. Doc Magovern had come to the house because Grampa was "having trouble with his blood." Now they were off to the hospital and I "wasn't to worry." This had happened before. Grampa had pernicious anemia and sometimes was very sick. So, naturally, it worried the pants off me. I actually thought about taking my bike down the dreaded 9N the three miles to the Saratoga

Hospital. Instead, I did as I knew they wanted. I opened the store and waited for customers. None came, though, and my eye was caught by the basketball stowed away as usual behind the door. I had to do something to take my mind off what was happening to Grampa. I took out the ball and went around the side.

When I started, I wasn't thinking about playing a game. My one thought was "If I make this one, Grampa is going to come home." Then I hit a two-handed shot from the foul line we'd scratched on the cracked black top. Not only that, for once the ball actually bounced straight back to me.

"If I make two in a row," I whispered to myself, "Grampa is going to live for . . . two more years." Then I took four steps back and put up an awkward left-hand hook. It hit the side of the building, scraped off the rough shingles, rattled around the rim and fell through. Two in a row! I took a deep breath. My heart was in my throat as my fingertips stroked the rough texture of the orange ball's surface. Some superstitious part of me felt as if I was holding my grandfather's life in my hands.

"If I make this one," I said out loud, "Grampa is going to live for another ten years." Then I tried my special trick shot. I threw the ball down as hard as I could onto that flat piece of pavement. It thwanged off the blacktop as if it was alive, so high that it was actually above the roof of the store. It flew in a rainbow arc, down, down, *Swish!* Straight through without touching the rim.

I raised both my fists up in the air. "Yes!" I shouted.

It would've been better if I'd kept my hands down. The ball richocheted off the rough surface and flew past me so fast that all I could do was hit it with my knee as I tried in vain to grab it before it reached the slanted part of the drive way.

Thwonk! Thwonk! It was picking up speed, the distance between bounces getting bigger while I watched with my mouth open. *Thwonk!* One huge final bounce as it soared into the uphill lane of 9N.

Whomp! I felt as much as heard the impact between the ball and the Eggleston Transport truck speeding north toward Corinth. The ball didn't bounce off, but lodged in the wide grill. And the driver of the big rig, who probably never even saw it, just kept going—taking my basketball and my wish with him.

And all I could do was smile.

Three hours later, Grampa and Grama pulled into the driveway in their old blue Plymouth with Grampa Jesse behind the wheel. He looked a little tired, but wasn't so pale now that they'd given him a transfusion. They both hugged me and thanked me for being so responsible and taking care of the store.

"We got time for a game a HORSE before supper," Grampa said. "It's getting dusk, but I could turn on the side lights."

I shook my head. "Let's just watch *Gunsmoke*," I said.

Somehow, my grandparents never noticed that the basketball was gone. And I didn't mind. The way I'd lost that ball had been like a sacrifice, a transaction in which I gave up a childish dream in exchange for something more important. I felt—satisfied.

I did get my growth—enough of it so that I stood 6'2" tall my senior year in high school. However, my grandfather never saw me play basketball on a team. No, it wasn't because my wish for his survival failed. Instead, I'd discovered a sport I truly was good at, its season the same time as basketball—

wrestling. My senior year in high school I was the varsity heavyweight and actually won the Regional Tournament while my grinning grandfather watched in the stands, telling everyone within earshot, "That's my grandson."

☆ *Lynea Bowdish* ☆

Lynea Bowdish grew up in Brooklyn, New York, where the most common sports were stick ball (played in the street), and stoop ball (played against the front stoop). No one seemed to mind not having uniforms, or teams, or regularly scheduled games with parents on the sidelines. The game started when someone came outside with a ball. It ended when most of the kids had been called home to dinner.

That doesn't mean Lynea doesn't like organized sports. She loves swimming and enjoys watching hockey (except for the fighting). Having grown up as one of the "large" kids, she also firmly believes that bird watching and computer games should qualify as sports when it comes to school fitness tests.

Lynea now lives in Maryland with her husband, David Roberts, and their two dogs, Zephyr and Cody.

Fat Girls ~~Can't~~ *Don't* Run

by

Lynea Bowdish

You're not supposed to call people "fat" anymore.
Instead, you're supposed to use words like "large," and
"big." As in, "wow, does she look large in those jeans."
Or "no one will ever date a girl that big."

You're not supposed to make fun of them, either.
The Tonight Show's Jay Leno doesn't know that. Neither
does the sixth grade class of Brookhaven Middle School.
They both make fun of fat people.

I'm "large." I'm also in sixth grade at Brookhaven Middle. Those two things don't go together.

"You're not really fat," Beverly says. "You'll grow out of it."

Beverly is my best friend, and when she says it, I almost believe her. Everyone believes Beverly. Even Ms. Sanchez, the gym teacher.

"I have a headache," Beverly tells Ms. Sanchez.

And because Beverly doesn't lie, she gets an excused absence.

When you're fat, everyone thinks you're making up excuses. And I do. So far this year I've tried a stomachache, blurry vision, a sick dog at home (his name is Henry), and a cold.

Nothing.

I really do try in gym. I grab the climbing rope and pull, but no matter how much Ms. Sanchez yells "Climb, Carla, climb," I can't.

That's me. Carla Anders.

I can't climb, and I can't sink a basketball. And I can't turn somersaults. My neck wasn't made to bend under my body. Not unless it were severely broken.

I'm not the only fat girl in sixth grade. But it's a question of degree.

Some are just slightly rounded, like Emily. But she's rounded in all the important places.

Some are thick and hard. They can pick up a desk with one hand, and would beat up anyone who called them fat.

And then there's Glenda and me.

Glenda and I don't talk, of course. That's one of the rules for being fat.

Fat kids don't talk to each other. Some of their weight might rub off on you and make you more noticeable. And the point is to stay as invisible as possible.

Which is why gym is so bad. It's impossible to be invisible in gym. Especially when you're trying to climb into gym shorts in the locker room.

No, I don't diet. When I was ten I tried a diet and gained five pounds. I gave up dieting forever.

And I don't exercise. The closest I get to exercise is Henry. I walk Henry every day after school. I love that dog. He's nine years old, and big and hairy, and he plods along and sniffs everything.

But sometimes Henry forgets he's nine. He begins to run. Henry's strong, so if I don't want to fall over, I have to run with him. Then after a while he remembers he's nine, and we go back to plodding.

I don't think walking your dog is considered exercise.

Anyway, last Monday Ms. Sanchez told us the sixth grade had to have physical fitness tests. I wondered what Glenda was feeling. I at least have friends, like Beverly and Emily, to cheer me up. Even Maya waves to me once in a while. Maya is the star athlete of the sixth grade. I've never heard Maya make fun of me. And so when Maya waves, I wave back. But Glenda has no friends.

Rope climbing was first. When my turn came, I grabbed the rope, hung on for dear life, and tried to get my feet off the floor. Instead, my hands slipped down the rope, and my palms burned.

I heard a few giggles, and Ms. Sanchez wrote something down on a clipboard. Beverly waved from the bleachers, where she sat with a stuffy nose.

Glenda was next, but couldn't do it.

Maya moved into place and scurried halfway to the ceiling before wriggling down.

The somersaults came next. I couldn't bear the thought of breaking my neck in two, so instead of pushing myself over, I fell to the side. When Ms. Sanchez pointed to Glenda, she just shook her head.

We moved to the basketball hoop (my throw didn't reach the hoop), then to the broad jump (I jumped two inches).

The final test was running around the sides of the gym. Two girls ran at a time. They supposedly were running against the clock, but everyone felt like they were competing against each other.

Glenda was paired with Emily. Emily came in first, but Glenda didn't do so badly.

I was paired with Maya, and our pair was last. Maya, star athlete, versus me.

As we stepped up to the line, Maya gave me a thumbs up. I tried to smile.

Ms. Sanchez blew the whistle, and we were off.

The first side wasn't so bad. Maya and I paced each other, and I almost enjoyed it.

The first corner came up and we rounded it together. That's when I started dropping back.

Was the rest of the class laughing? Was I jiggling?

The second corner went by. Maybe I should focus. I pictured Henry and me, and Henry breaking into a run. He was pulling me. My legs strained to keep up with him.

Maya was in front of me, but not that far.

As I rounded the third corner, I inched up on Maya and then went past her. Suddenly I felt the power of possibility, and it felt good. Could I win?

Maya was a few steps behind me now. Down at the end of the gym, I could see Ms. Sanchez and her stopwatch. Beverly was jumping up and down, and the rest of the class—were they cheering?

At that moment, I knew I really wanted to come in first. Maybe just once in my life I could win.

I bet you think I'm going to tell you I won. Well, this isn't that kind of a story. It wouldn't be very realistic, would it? No, at that moment, Maya moved ahead.

The next thing I knew, I was slamming into the wall. I put my hands on my knees and tried to breathe. Then I slumped down against the wall next to Maya. She was panting, too, and sweating, and laughing.

"That was great," she gasped.

"Yeah, it was," I said.

I was surprised. I actually meant it. It had been great.

I remembered the moment when I had moved ahead, and when I thought I might win. I felt a glow just thinking about it. I had run a good race. It felt wonderful.

"I didn't know you could run," Maya said.

"Neither did I," I said.

"We're starting a girls track team," Maya said. "Interested?"

Was I? Definitely.

Maybe it isn't that fat girls can't run. Maybe it's that they don't run. Because if they do run, they have to ignore the jokes and the giggles.

But from now on, I would run. Because I wanted to.

I wondered about Glenda. She had run a good race, too. Maybe she'd be interested in the track team.

Beverly sat down next to us and gave me a hug.

"Great race," Beverly said. "I didn't know you could run."

"I didn't know, either," I said.

Then I laughed.

"But Henry did."

☆ *David Lubar* ☆

David Lubar grew up in Morristown, New Jersey. He's written seventeen books and close to 200 short stories for teens and young readers. He has designed a lot of video games, including *Home Alone* and *Frogger 2* for the GameBoy. His books include  *Punished!*, *Hidden Talents*, and *The Curse of the Campfire Weenies and Other Warped and Creepy Tales*.

He wrote "Bounce-back" because he played a lot of table tennis when he was young. Back then, everyone wanted to play against him, because he was so easy to beat. He still isn't very good. You could probably beat him. So could your dog or little sister. If you want to learn which other sports he is especially bad at, check out his story "Two Left Hands, Two Left Feet, and Too Left on the Bench" in Darby Creek's anthology, *Sports Shorts*.

Bounce-Back

by

David Lubar

"Wow, that's huge." Tyler stopped dead in his tracks and stared up at the gleaming gold trophy. It sat on a table in the lobby of the YMCA. A sign on the wall behind the table read, "Ping-Pong tournament next week." Until that moment, Tyler hadn't cared all that much about Ping-Pong, but the sight of the trophy made the game a whole lot more interesting. Tyler had never won a trophy—not even a tiny one.

"Hey, wait up," his friend Bobby called as he came out of the locker room.

Tyler dashed over and started talking, hoping to distract Bobby so he wouldn't notice the trophy. Tyler didn't want any extra competition. But before Tyler could speak five words, Bobby stopped dead in his tracks, stared at the trophy, and said, "Wow, that's huge."

"It's not that big," Tyler said, trying to move between Bobby and the sign.

"Cool—check out the sign," Bobby said. "There's a tournament. I'm going to enter. How about you?"

Tyler shrugged, but didn't say anything.

"I've got a Ping-Pong table," Bobby said. "Why don't you come over? We can practice together."

Tyler almost said yes. Then he realized something. *If we practice, I'll get better. But so will Bobby.*

"Well?" Bobby asked.

"Maybe tomorrow," Tyler said. He headed home and went right to the basement. There it was, shoved against the back wall under a dozen cardboard boxes filled with old clothes, two boxes of empty pickle jars, three ancient computers that didn't work, and count-less back issues of *National Geographic*. There it was—a Ping-Pong table.

A sweaty hour later, Tyler had cleared off the boxes and pulled the table away from the wall. *Bobby's in for a surprise.* Tyler grinned at the thought of winning the tournament.

He ran upstairs and asked his big brother, "Will you play Ping-Pong with me?"

"Can't," his brother said. "I have to write a paper for school."

He asked his mom when she got home from her office. "I'd love to," she said, "but I have a lot of extra work to take care of this week."

He asked his dad when he got home from his job. "I'd really like to, but I need to pack for my business trip."

As Tyler sighed and walked away, his dad said, "Why don't you set it up to play against yourself?"

"I can do that?" Tyler asked.

"Sure." His dad headed for the basement steps. "Come on. I'll show you."

When they got downstairs, Tyler's dad folded one side of the table so it stuck straight up, meeting the other half like a wall meets a floor. "There you go. Hit the ball into that and it will bounce back so you can hit it again."

"Thanks." Tyler grabbed a paddle and walked over to the side that wasn't folded up. He hit the ball against the upright side. It bounced back and flew past him before he could take a swing at it. He chased after the ball and tried again, with exactly the same results.

For the next two hours, Tyler mostly got practice in bending down and picking the ball up from the floor. But he kept trying. After a while, he was able to hit the ball as it shot back at him, though it didn't always go where he wanted. Then he started hitting it two or three times in a row. Finally, he was able to keep it going, hitting the ball hard and fast, smashing it again and again into the upright half of the table as he dreamed about how nice the trophy would look in his bedroom.

The next day, after their basketball league, Bobby asked Tyler, "So, want to come practice Ping-Pong today?"

"No thanks," Tyler said.

"Come on. The only person who will play with me is my big sister. And she keeps beating me."

"Maybe tomorrow," Tyler said. But he had no plans to practice with anyone else—not now that he'd found such a great way to turn himself into an awesome Ping-Pong champ. For the rest of the week, he spent hours every day slamming the ball against the bounce-back, getting faster and faster with his paddle.

"I am unbeatable," he said as he finished his last session the morning of the tournament.

Tyler headed for the YMCA.

"Hey, are you playing?" Bobby asked when Tyler walked into the gym. "I thought you weren't interested."

"I figured I'd give it a shot," Tyler said. He looked across the gym. The trophy had been brought in from the lobby. It glistened in the light, as if it were winking at him. "Are you playing?"

Bobby shrugged. "Sure. Why not. I've gotten a bit better. I'm still not too good, but it should be fun."

"Yeah," Tyler said, "it should be lots of fun."

Tyler was delighted to learn that his first opponent was Bobby. It would be nice to start the tournament with an easy win. "Go ahead," Tyler said. "You can serve." It didn't matter who served first. Either way, Tyler knew it would be a quick game.

Bobby picked up the ball. "Ready."

Tyler nodded. "You bet." He could already taste his stunning victory. He hoped Bobby would be a good sport about losing.

"Watch out. I've been practicing," Bobby said.

"Thanks for the warning," Tyler said.

Clack. Bobby served the ball. Tyler, feeling fast and loose, swung his paddle in a lightning-quick smashing return stroke, just like he'd done all week in his basement.

He swung so hard, his whole body spun around. When he finished his spin, he looked back at the table. Bobby's slow serve was just coming over the net. *Plink.* It bounced once. *Plink.* It bounced a second time.

"My point," Bobby said. He served again. Tyler swung hard and fast again. And way too soon again.

After Tyler lost the first five points, it was his turn to serve. That didn't help. He kept hitting the ball too hard and missing the table. Five more lost points, and it was Bobby's serve.

The game was over before Tyler knew what had happened. Bobby won a stunning victory, twenty-one to three. Tyler was just too fast.

"Nice try," Bobby said as Tyler was leaving the gym. "But can I give you some advice?"

"What?" Tyler asked as he glanced over his shoulder for one last look at the golden trophy that would never be his.

"Maybe next time you should practice. It might help."

☆ *Terry Trueman* ☆

As a preteen, Terry Trueman considered himself a tremendous athlete, playing sports constantly in his neighborhood in the northern suburbs of Seattle, Washington. Only as he got into high school did he discover that his calling in life was not professional sports but

typing poems, short stories, and novels in his basement with two fingers (he never took a typing or keyboarding class). Trueman does not regret the change in career directions, but his fanatical love of sports morphed into an almost psychotic 'fanhood' of all Seattle/Pacific Northwest teams (the Mariners, Seahawks, UW Huskies football, and Gonzaga hoops). Terry Trueman lives in Spokane, Washington, and travels the world extensively, talking about writing and watching ESPN every night in his hotel room. His wife, Patti, can usually handle his sports TV addiction . . . usually.

H-O-R-S-E

by

Terry Trueman

I'm twelve years old, and Brad Slater and I have played . . . I don't know . . . maybe ten million games of HORSE in our lives. We're playing right now. If you don't know, HORSE is a basketball game, usually played between two players, where player 1 makes a shot and player 2 has to make that same shot. If you make the shot, whatever shot you like, a lay-in or a long shot, then it's your turn to shoot first again and your opponent has to make the same shot as you. If player 2 misses he gets a letter, first miss an H, second miss an O and so on until you've spelled out HORSE, at which time the game is over and you've lost. If you don't have much time you can play PIG; if you're vulgar you can play the game by spelling out some obscene or profane swear word. Unlike regular basketball, HORSE doesn't require dry pavement to dribble on or sidelines to keep you in bounds, no rebounding or assists, steals or traveling violations; it doesn't demand anything other than a ball, a hoop and two or more players.

> *I've never beat Brad before,*
> *never,*
> *ever,*
> *E-V-E-R*
> *at HORSE,*
> *at PIG*

or any other
version of the game with
any other word.
Truthfully,
come to think of it,
I've never beaten Brad
at anything *athletic.*
But today
I'm up over
Brad's
H-O-R-S
with my
H-O.
It's like a
good poem,
no
it's
a great poem
a perfect poem,
a rare and nearly impossible and
utterly
unimaginably, divine poem.

I'm beating
Brad Slater—
I never, ever
thought
this could
happen.

Dry leaves skitter along
the asphalt;
the breeze
blows in my face.
My feet
tingle in my
athletic shoes
H-O-R-S
to
H-O . . .

"Your shot," Brad says
tossing me the ball.
I catch it,
smile, set up

fifteen feet away,
and
launch my
fade-away
jumper . . .

Swish.

Brad grabs the rebound
walks to my
spot,
takes a few deep
breaths,
judges distance,
wind,
humidity,
takes another
deep breath
and finally
lets fly—
the ball
almost goes through

but circles the hoop and
rims out.
That's E for Brad
H-O-R-S-E.

The way we play, after the final letter in HORSE, the loser gets to choose whether to take the shot again or make the winner repeat the shot, making it a second time; it's like having to win by two points in Ping-Pong or volleyball or tennis—a confident player usually tries the shot a second time, and Brad is nothing if not confident, but today, now, a fifteen foot fade-away jumper is not an easy shot—Brad eyes the distance again and then . . .

"Prove it," he says
throwing me the ball.
I stand
fifteen feet
from the hoop. . .

This length of jumper,
much less a fade-away jumper,
is a hard shot;
he thinks I'll miss.

But
suddenly
a Robin flies
over our heads
twittering,
his eye
staring
straight into my eyes
I think he's
smiling,
and the grey clouds
move
so slowly
that I'm sure
the sky,
silent,
watches us—

I
grab the ball
and
don't let myself think
about . . .

> You have to make it
> You have to win
> Nothing
> in the world
> can stop you now
> for once
> in this single moment
> you
> can't lose,
> not this time . . .

No,
all these thoughts
may come later,
if I make it,
But for now
I grab the ball,

hold it
lightly
in my skinny fingers,
glance at the hoop
and
I leap,
rising high
into the air
raising my arms above
my head
as though offering
this shot to
God,
and I fade away
like a man falling
from a high cliff,
like a song's last refrains
like
the way one's
breath must
finally seize
at the hour of one's

death—
And from this fading
falling, flying
I
shoot—

A tiny click
as the ball nicks the
metal hoop
yet slams
through!

All the universe is
silence
except for the ball
bouncing
once,
twice, a third time
and a fourth
each bounce smaller than
the one before it
Bounce---bounce--bounce-bounce-bounce-bounce

until it lies,
motionless, on the
dark ground.

"You win"
Brad says,
trying to sound
relaxed and cool.
Now, quickly
"Wanna play again?"
I almost say,
sure,
but the word catches in my throat
"Nah, I gotta get home."
"Really?" Brad asks
I'm almost certain
I can hear
pain,
pain,
P-A-I-N
in his voice.
"Yeah," I say,

staring right at him
"We'll play again
tomorrow."
"Okay" Brad says
feigning
calm,
faking
indifference,
"See you tomorrow then,"
he says,
his tone
anguished.
I say
"Okay."

I hold my
smile
until I'm out of his sight.
then the breeze
blows in my hair;
my feet dance
as I walk

six inches above the earth.
My heart beats
with the strangest rhythm,
one I've never
felt before:
pride,
joy,
victory—
I am twelve
years old
and I don't
realize
that
nothing,
nothing,
n-o-t-h-i-n-g—nothing
will ever
taste
this sweet
again.

☆ *CS Perryess* ☆

When CS Perryess is writing, he can never predict who's going to walk onto the page. The day Amanda Jackson showed up, he recognized her as an alternate version of a much-appreciated BMX-riding former student. He was pleased to discover that as the

story moved along, Amanda grew into someone with the potential to be as strong and wonderful as the student he remembers so fondly.

CS Perryess has a great life in a foggy little California town with his wonderful wife, Ellen, a stream ecologist and volunteer at the local animal shelter. He rides his bike to work, to the local farmers' market, and every so often to the hardware store where people laugh at him when he's lashing ten-foot lengths of pipe to the bike frame.

Amazing Dirt Girl Rides Again

by

CS Perryess

"Fine! I hate you!" Kinsey screams.

At me, her used-to-be-best-friend—Amanda Jackson: third row, second seat, the only seventh-grade girl with the Nukeproof hubset on her desk.

Everybody knows now. Even Jeremy.

Mrs. Angelo bursts in, yelling, "Kinsey Wilkinson!"

I almost hear her send Kinsey to the office. I almost hear Kinsey slam the door, but I'm pushing my face hard into the desktop. I'm covering both ears. How could I say something that mean to my best friend in the whole world, forever?

I know Jeremy's looking straight at me and that perfect, new Nukeproof hubset. Every piece of my skin is about two hundred degrees. That fake wood stuff on the desk feels cold.

Yesterday Kinsey and me hung at the mall. Yesterday she was the only one who knew my secret— I still ride. She told me she liked Ben Ranzini. We laughed about Jeremy's hairy legs. We tiptoed into Sport-o-Rama to check out the BMX stuff. I told her about last week's County Dirt Comps and that tweaked landing—how my bike needs a new hubset. Yesterday, Kinsey and me were best friends.

"There will be no more outbursts." It's the first thing I really hear. Mrs. Angelo's big flat hand pats my steaming back. She starts in where she left off yesterday—the Crusades—all these people getting killed for God and nutmeg. I hate pumpkin pie.

I know, right now Jeremy is looking at the hub-set. He knows I still ride. He'll drop me.

How come I went and unwrapped it here in class? I can't believe it. She got me a Nukeproof X-06. It must've cost her a chunk.

Something pokes my arm—must be Derek in front of me with that stupid mechanical pencil. I pull my arms in.

Ow! I will not look up.

Ow. How's he doing that?

Ow again! This glowy flitty thing worms its way between my wrist and the desk.

Whamo!

Everything changes: The classroom noises are history. I don't even know what's going on.

"Yo," says this ticked-off twinky voice.

My eyes are so shut I see those blood-spark things in my eyelids.

"Yo!" the twinky voice says again.

I know that voice.

"Yo. Mandyface."

Zoe. That's what Zoe calls me—or used to call me way back when I invented her. She disappeared when I learned about hormones in fifth grade. Somehow imaginary friends and feminine hygiene products just didn't work together.

That same year I won the Under-twelve Regional BMX Dirt Comps. The paper called me "Amazing Dirt Girl"—major social drag.

I sneak one eye open.

"Made ya look!" Zoe pulls a tailwhip in the air.

I open both eyes. She pedals off—out toward Derek. But Derek and his greasy neck aren't there, and Jeremy isn't there, and Mrs. Angelo isn't drawing trade routes on the board. In fact, there is no board. I sit up.

Everything's hot and dry and sandy. The hubset floats nearby, and there's Zoe, zooming around in front of me like always—or like I imagined back when I was little.

What's the deal?

I mean, where am I? How come I can see Zoe? She cranks a wicked infinity roll and lands on my thumb.

"You look ticked," she says, pulling off her helmet.

Zoe looks me right in the eye. It's weird seeing her. I mean, I always imagined she had little wings and a killer bike and she looked just like me, only she had more guts, more *chutzpa* like Uncle Morris says. Only now she's got more me, too. I mean in fifth grade there wasn't much me, and now there's more, if you get what I'm saying. So now there's more of her, too. Only how could there be more of somebody who's not real?

The glitter sparkles on her tricked-out bike.

"I said the worst thing in the world to Kinsey, and now she hates me," I say.

"Hold up," she says, "I've been incognito a while. Isn't Kinsey the dweeby one with the braids?"

"She's my best friend in the whole world, forever," I say, remembering those stupid braids she used to wear, and how skinny she was—not model-skinny, more like geeky-skinny. "She's different now," I say. Yeah, different enough so three high school guys were sneaking through the perfume aisle at Mervyn's to get a look at her.

Zoe straps on her helmet and pulls an air-180 over the sand. "So what part's real?" she says, "The best friend part or the hate part?"

Zoe is asking me what's real? This whole thing is getting too zoney for me. I turn and look around. Now Zoe's busting a superman seat-grab over the dusty desert. She speeds past these camels and a bunch of guys dressed in bathrobes, then circles back to my thumb.

"So?" She taps her foot.

"The Nukeproof hubset," I say. It floats next to us over the dunes, gleaming black and silver. "Kinsey gave it to me."

"Cool."

"Well," I say, "Yeah."

"So?"

"In front of everybody—even Jeremy. I mean he's really going to like a dirty BMX punk-girl. Jeremy hates it when girls do guy stuff."

Zoe manhandles a 360 tailwhip up by my face and knocks on my head. "Hello." She says. Her Nukeproof X-06s gleam.

"Mandyface," she says. "Your old set's busted. Your best friend gets you a new one. Best friend in the world, forever. This Jeremy chump can't even ride."

She pulls a squeaker across the Nukeproof logo, then flies off into a sandstorm.

Whamo!

I'm back in class.

"…travelers in a foreign land, exploring new social rules for which they were unprepared," says Mrs. Angelo. "Every turn involved difficult choices. Nonetheless, they persevered."

Everybody's taking notes, even Derek. My new hubset feels solid and heavy in my hand.

I stand.

"Amanda?"

"May I please go to the office?"

She nods.

I walk right past Jeremy, who doesn't look so good. I flash my new hubset and smile. The gel in his hair is clumped by his left ear. There's a zit I never saw before on his forehead.

I absolutely have to tell Kinsey I didn't mean it.

Maybe I can get to the office before Kinsey gets detention for life.

Maybe I can make things right.

Maybe I could let people know I'm one of the best riders in three counties.

Maybe that's okay.

Maybe Jeremy's wrong.

Of course Kinsey bought me a new hubset. Of course she'll understand. Kinsey is my best friend in the world, forever.

☆ *Dorian Cirrone* ☆

Although the story "Riding the Wave" isn't entirely auto-biographical, Dorian Cirrone still remembers Sammy the surfer vividly, many years after she first watched him surfing on Sunny Isles Beach in south Florida. She also remembers trying to surf and

falling off the board most of the time, even with her brother Chris's help.

Cirrone has written many other works for children and adults. Her story, "Finding High Jump Fame: A Shorts Story," was featured in the Darby Creek anthology *Sports Shorts*. In addition, she is the author of two teen novels, *Dancing in Red Shoes Will Kill You* and *Prom Kings and Drama Queens*; as well as the Lindy Blues mysteries, *The Missing Silver Dollar* and *The Big Scoop*. You can visit her website at www.doriancirrone.com.

Riding the Wave

by

Dorian Cirrone

"C'mon, get off your butt!" my brother, Chris, said. "I'll teach you how to surf."

I held my hand above my eyes and squinted up at him from my beach towel. "I'm working on my tan," I said.

He frowned. "Don't be so lazy."

It was summer vacation and we'd both been spending a lot of time at Sunny Isles Beach, along with everyone else who hadn't gone to camp or summer school. "I'm not lazy," I said. "Just comfortable right now." I loved the feel of the hot sun on my face and the rushing sound of the waves as they rolled onto the shore. I was happy not moving a muscle. I even liked the rotting fish smell of the seaweed strewn along the shore.

Chris threw his surfboard in the sand next to me and plopped himself down in the middle of it. "It'll be fun," he said, picking up my suntan lotion and squirting it on my leg.

I sat up and scowled at him. "What's wrong? No surfing buddies to hang out with?" Although he was thirteen and I was fourteen, we had little in common and rarely spent time together. Even when we were at the beach, we hardly crossed each other's paths. He was usually out in the water paddling around, while I was on the beach reading or sunbathing. I figured he must have been really bored.

He picked up a handful of sand and let it sift slowly through his fingers. "Everyone must be out of town or something."

I rubbed the suntan lotion onto my leg and squirted some on the other one, savoring the coconut scent. "They've probably all been carted off to the home for annoying adolescent boys—I can't believe they missed you."

"Very funny," Chris said, "you should do stand-up comedy, except that you'd probably be too lazy to stand up."

I rolled my eyes. "I told you; I'm not lazy. I just don't see the fun in spending your time battling against the waves to paddle out, and then sitting there for who-knows-how-long until a good enough wave comes by. Then for about one second you get to ride on the stupid board before you fall into the ocean, possibly inhaling enough saltwater to boil a pot of spaghetti."

My brother ignored my rant. He had apparently forgotten the previous time he tried to teach me to surf. I'd hoisted my bottom-heavy body onto the board and struggled to paddle out. I was one of those girls with a pear-shaped figure and no arm strength at all.

In PE when we had to hang with our chin above the bar for the fitness test, I usually lasted about half a second. When I tried to surf, I couldn't even paddle hard enough with the waves in order to catch one and ride it to the shore. I was about to decline my brother's invitation one more time when something caught my eye behind him.

It was a guy who looked a little older than we were, someone I'd never seen before. He carried his surfboard under his arm like every other surfer, but in between the board and his body was a metal crutch. He had a second crutch on the other side. The muscles in his arms rippled as he struggled against the sand that threatened to swallow the bottoms of the crutches. Between the metal, one good leg hopped toward the water while the other dangled in the air, withered and gnarled into a permanently twisted position.

My brother turned to see what I was looking at.

"Dude," the guy said, "how are the waves?"

"Goin' off," Chris answered, as the guy passed us.

"Who's that?" I asked.

"His name's Sammy," Chris said. "He usually surfs on the other side of the pier."

"How can he surf?"

Chris smiled. "You'd be surprised."

I watched as Sammy threw his crutches onto the shore and hopped a few feet to the water's edge. He threw the board into the water and gently belly flopped onto it. Slicing the surface of the water, his massive arms propelled him as he battled against the waves. His crutches glinted in the sunlight as he moved farther and farther away from them.

I continued to study him as he maneuvered the board around and straddled it, facing the shore. He turned his head back, watching and waiting patiently for a wave to catch. After a few minutes, he spun forward and slammed his stomach down onto the board for take-off. He paddled furiously.

"Watch his moves," Chris said.

But I was barely listening, mesmerized by the elegance of the surfboard and Sammy working together as one. Suddenly he was riding the wave, rising on one leg, the other mangled one wafting in the wind. The white foam curled behind him as he stood with his arms outstretched to the sides.

Deep within me, I could feel what Sammy must have felt, the majesty of those moments as he sailed toward the shore. He was free. Free from his handicap, from his crutches, from all the limitations he endured on land.

I felt ashamed of my own laziness, of the boundaries I'd carved out for myself just because I couldn't hang from a bar or because my hips were bigger than those of the other girls.

I turned to Chris. "Get up."

He looked at me puzzled, but obeyed. I grabbed his surfboard and began flopping in the sand, running toward the water with my brother behind me. I knew I'd never look as graceful as Sammy had, but I didn't care. "Surf's up!" I yelled as I threw the board into the water and headed toward the horizon.

☆ *Jamie McEwan* ☆

Jamie McEwan lives in Connecticut with his wife, the celebrated Sandra Boynton, and their four children. He is the author of six books for children, including the Scrubs series for Darby Creek (*Willy the Scrub*, *Whitewater Scrubs*, *Rufus the*  *Scrub Does* <u>Not</u> *Wear a Tutu*, and *Scrubs Forever*).

Although Jamie was mediocre at best on the usual school teams—football, soccer, baseball—he was lucky enough to discover a couple of more compatible sports. Captain of his high school and college wrestling teams, Jamie was also a two-time Olympian in whitewater canoe slalom, winning a bronze medal in singles in 1972 and returning twenty years later to place fourth with doubles partner Lecky Haller. He has paddled the rivers of seventeen different countries around the world. And only once did he lose his shorts.

Red Shorts, White Water

by

Jamie McEwan

First of all, to help you understand this story better, I want to describe the shorts.

Not that there was anything terribly special about the shorts. They were my dad's old soccer shorts, red, with double white stripes down the sides and a white *M* on one thigh. He had worn them back when he was a college soccer star. The red was pretty faded, and they had lost their string, and the elastic was a little stretched out, and they were big on me. But I liked them. My dad had played varsity games in those shorts. He had scored goals. I thought it was kind of cool to wear those baggy old things around.

I hadn't started the day wearing them. I was hanging around the house on this summer Saturday morning in jeans and a T-shirt when the phone rang. It was my friend, Justin Hardy. Justin was a quiet guy, two grades ahead of me, who spent most of his free time playing his Les Paul guitar. But we did have one thing in common.

"Hey, Ted," said Justin, "you know that rain yesterday?"

"Yeah?" I hadn't been outside yet. I looked out the window at yesterday's clouds being blown to pieces. Bright blue sky showed through the gaps.

"It brought the Pagan way up," said Justin.

"Oh, yeah?"

"You want to run it?"

"Maybe." I had kayaked the Pagan River before, and I knew it would be fun. But I was feeling lazy. And I also knew it was a long walk from the road to get to the good part—a long walk if you were lugging a kayak, that is.

"Come on, Ted," said Justin. "Jodie's in. And my cousin wants to watch us do it. You met her—Melissa. She's never seen us kayak."

I remembered Melissa, all right: my height, brown hair, brown eyes, nice smile.

"Uh . . . yeah. Sure, why not?"

Nobody kayaks in jeans. I changed into those shorts I told you about, grabbed my paddle and helmet and life jacket and sprayskirt, and dragged my boat from the garage onto the lawn. I was waiting there when Justin and Melissa and our friend Jodie drove up.

The Pagan River was running browner and higher than I'd ever seen it. I was a little nervous at first, especially since I didn't have exactly the right boat for it. The only kayaks we had were what they call "play boats," made for river surfing and doing tricks. They look more like big plastic potato chips than like kayaks—potato chips with bubbles in the middle, where the deck is high enough to fit your knees under.

It wasn't long before I mostly got over being nervous. We were careful. We would paddle one rapid at a time, then get out to look over the next one. This made it easy for Melissa, who was on foot, to keep up.

There was no path, so she was scrambling along the bank, ducking under branches, hopping from rock to rock. Some people would have been annoyed, or bored, or both, but no, she was into it, clapping and cheering us on in the harder rapids. She was wearing hiking boots, and khaki shorts, and a flannel shirt with the sleeves cut off, and she looked pretty great.

Near the end of the run we came to the biggest rapid, the one we called "Barbed Wire," because of a stretch of old fence along the shore. We got out of our kayaks and climbed up the bank to take a look. The water slid over a smooth, wide ledge of stone, fell at about a forty-five degree angle, then kicked up into a couple of good-sized waves as it flowed into the deep pool below. It was a good drop, though pretty straightforward.

But I saw another possibility. "Hey, look," I said, pointing. "The water's high enough, you could take that route on the left."

"Straight into the shore," said Jodie.

"No, you make a big turn, then down that sort of ramp, there."

"Maybe," said Jodie. "I like the straight way. Direct. That's the kind of girl I am."

We laughed. Jodie was short, and muscular, and athletic, and yes, pretty direct.

Justin and Melissa and I watched as Jodie launched herself off the drop, disappeared for a moment into the big wave at the bottom, and then surfaced in the slower water.

"Yee-ha!" shouted Jodie, raising her paddle over her head.

"My turn," said Justin as he fitted himself into his kayak. And then over he went, too, down the drop, through the wave, into the pool below.

"They make it look easy," Melissa said to me.

"Yeah. It is pretty easy."

"Are you going to try that other way?"

I hadn't planned to, until she asked. But she sounded so hopeful.

"Sure. I don't want you to get bored," I said.

"All right!" she said, nodding.

I was feeling happy and excited as I slid into the cockpit of my kayak and snapped on my sprayskirt. I didn't say, "Okay, watch this!" as I pushed off into the current. I was thinking it, though.

It's hard to say why I wanted to impress Melissa. She was Justin's age, two years older than I was. And she was only visiting for a week or two. So I didn't have the slightest thought that I was going to go out with her or anything. But, well, I just did, I wanted to impress her. I wanted to do something different. Something just a little bit daring.

I'd never had anybody to impress before, kayaking. It didn't do any good to try to impress Jodie; she was a lot better than I was.

I gave Melissa a casual little wave as I started across. Then I tried to forget all about her. I tried to concentrate on the job at hand.

I was heading across the narrow river, aiming almost at the opposite bank. I got myself on the jet of current that was flowing that way and let it carry me with it. Easy enough. But then the current slowed down and doubled back on itself, turning almost 180 degrees. I took a big back stroke that spun me around, too.

As I turned I could feel the back of my boat go underwater. I could feel this because it changed the way the rest of the boat felt; it made the bow rise and wobble. But this didn't matter—I thought—because I was sure the stern would pop up again in a moment, and I would go merrily on my way.

But the stern didn't pop up. In fact, it went further down. And then my bow sank, too.

I couldn't understand it. Somehow my whole boat was sinking. At first I thought my sprayskirt must have popped off. But no—there was no water in the boat. My legs were still dry.

And yet now I had water flowing right over my head! I couldn't sink any more because I was stuck to the bottom of the river! Although there was no impact, I'd stopped moving. I was pasted against the bedrock like a leaf on a stone, held motionless while the river was flowing up my back and over my head, forcing me forward against the deck of my boat. When I resisted, pushing myself upright again, I could see through the spray flying over me, and I could breathe. I could see Melissa on the bank across from me. But it was a big effort to push myself back against the current. When I leaned forward again, to rest my back, my head went completely underwater.

This was bad.

I threw my weight back and forth, trying to dislodge the boat. Nothing.

I tried to plant my paddle on the rock, to push myself free. No way.

Okay. I'd tried Plan A, I'd tried Plan B—now what should I do?

It came to me in a flash: PANIC! Now I was going to panic, that's what I was going to do! I reached forward, tore off my sprayskirt, and wrenched myself out of the kayak, bruising myself in my hurry. I was out of there.

Now that I was loose, the water swept me away. I bumped down over the rest of the ledge, and then I was swimming.

Gasping and spluttering, I headed toward shore. Something was tangled in my feet, making it hard to swim. I could see Justin and Jodie, downstream. Melissa was running down to the water's edge. I got to where the water was calm; I started to stand up—and then I sat down again, as low as I could get.

My shorts! Where were my darned shorts?

I threw my paddle onto shore, ducked underwater, and reached down with both hands. I found that my shorts had been pulled all the way down to where they'd been stopped by my sandals. By one sandal, really. And so, while Melissa asked, over and over, "Are you okay? Are you okay?" I thrashed around in the shallows, trying to untangle my shorts and get my other foot through and pull them up again. I was sure glad the water was muddy.

Finally I got my shorts on again. And the boat floated loose; Justin and Jodie retrieved it, undamaged. And I still had my paddle. And I had my shorts back on. I was all right, apart from a couple of minor scrapes and bruises. No harm done.

At least, no physical harm.

"What were you doing, there, in the pool?" asked Justin. He'd just dragged my boat through the bushes back up to where I was standing, shaking the water out of my ears.

"Nothing," I said.

"No, really, what were you doing? It looked like you were fighting with something underwater."

"Nothing," repeated Melissa. I glanced at her. She wasn't smiling. Not even a little bit.

Justin gave both of us a funny look, but he didn't ask again. He turned away and walked back to his kayak.

Now Melissa allowed herself to smile. And laugh. I looked down at my feet. I could feel my face turning red.

"Hey, Ted," said Melissa. "Like you promised— I wasn't bored!"

That made me laugh, too. "Neither was I," I confessed.

End of story.

Oh—I gave the shorts back to my dad.

I make sure I wear shorts with a drawstring, now, when I go kayaking.

And I don't forget to tie them on.

☆ *Max Elliot Anderson* ☆

Max Elliot Anderson grew up as a reluctant reader. After surveying the market, he sensed the need for action-adventures and mysteries for readers ages eight to thirteen, especially boys.

Anderson has produced, directed, or shot over five hundred national television commercials for True Value Hardware Stores. He also won a best cinematographer award for the film *Pilgrim's Progress*.

Using his extensive experience in the production of motion pictures, videos, and television commercials, Anderson brings visual excitement and heart-pounding action to his stories. His unique characters, setting, and plot have led some young readers to compare reading one of Mr. Anderson's seven published books to being inside an exciting or scary movie.

Big Foot

by

Max Elliot Anderson

Nearly every town where Jeff Spencer had lived before came complete with a new bully. Jeff's father was a salesman, and he moved the family around a lot.

Then in the last place where they lived . . . Jeff's father died. That's why he and his mother moved back to Boulder Creek.

"You'll like it here," she told him. "I grew up in this town, and now you will too."

Unfortunately, Jeff had a big problem. And it wasn't the sort of thing a guy could easily hide. One look as he came ambling down the sidewalk, and a neighborhood bully was sure to pop out of the bushes any second.

Then it happened.

"Hey," a menacing voice called out.

Trying to act as tough as possible, Jeff answered, "Hey yourself."

"What's your name?" this frightening character demanded.

"Jeff. Jeff Spencer. What's yours?"

The boy first looked him straight in the eye. Then his eyes drifted down until he was staring at Jeff's feet. "People around here call me Denny. You a new kid or something?"

Jeff grinned. "No, I'm not new. I'll be thirteen on my next birthday." Jeff took a half step back. He thought about making a run for his house, but he knew he'd never make it. Then he looked back to Denny. "Me and my mom just moved in. Why?"

"I'll ask the questions around here," Denny threatened. Then he looked down again. "What's wrong with your foot?"

Jeff looked down and raised it slightly off the sidewalk. "This thing? I get around on it okay. Do you go to school near here?"

Why do you care?"

"Because I thought we might be in the same one. I'm goin' out for football this year."

Denny nearly doubled up with laughter. After he caught his breath he said, "Be serious. With a foot like that you can't run fast, or you'd have done that already." He slowly shook his head. "And you can't jump high, that's for sure." Jeff managed to leave without a fight.

In his new school Jeff heard some of the same comments as in all the other places he'd lived before. The worst part of his day happened as he walked from one class to the next. Guys lined both sides of the hallway just to watch him stumble along. Denny was their leader.

But this year, Jeff had a little surprise. He called it his secret weapon. Even his mother didn't know about it.

Then one afternoon, he spotted something on the bulletin board outside the football coach's office. Jeff read the words silently. *Attention! Football tryouts today! Meet on the practice field at four o'clock.*

He was just about to leave when a familiar voice taunted, "You gotta be kidding me," Denny scoffed.

Jeff turned around, expecting only to see Denny. He saw him all right, but it looked like the entire football team stood next to him. They began moving toward Jeff when Coach Davis came out of his office. "Hey. What's going on here?"

Denny raised his hands and cocked his head to one side. "Nothing."

Mr. Davis studied Denny and his friends for a moment and then turned to Jeff. "Is there a problem here?"

Jeff looked to the mob, and shook his head.

The coach folded his arms and looked back at the boys. "If you have anything to settle, take it out to the practice field." He pushed his way through the guys on either side of Denny.

Denny slowly nodded as he jammed his finger into Jeff's chest. "Yeah. Like Coach said. I'll see you on the practice field."

When the team manager handed out equipment, he had no trouble until he looked at Jeff's feet.

"I take a size nine for my left foot, and the biggest thing you got for my right."

The coach met him around the fifty-yard line. "You sure about this?" he asked. Jeff nodded, but no matter how hard he tried, it was impossible to keep up. Because he was so slow, the coach started him out at center. Denny took that opportunity to make sure he and his friends squashed Jeff like a bug.

All during the day, the team gave him a rough time in school, and at practices they made his life even more miserable.

Then at the end of practice on the Friday before their first game, the coach took Jeff to one side. The rest of the team continued working on drills and Denny practiced kicking field goals from the twenty-yard line.

"Listen, son," Coach began. "I admire the way you come out here, day after day, and take the kind of pounding these guys dish out. But why don't you think about becoming one of the managers?"

Jeff slowly shook his head, his voice cracked slightly as he said, "No sir."

"Be reasonable, Jeff. You can't run like the other guys, and you can't jump as high. There's not much more a player can do for a team than that."

"I wanna be the kicker."

"Nobody's gettin' my job," Denny threatened. "My dad was the kicker when he played here. So was my uncle."

"There's only one way to find out." The coach blew his whistle and announced, "Get me a ball." The team proceeded out to the twenty-yard line.

"Best out of five tries," the coach bellowed. Five times the ball was placed and five times Denny put it squarely between the uprights. After his final kick he shuffled off the field with pride.

"Spencer! You're next," Coach ordered.

Jeff stepped forward. "Coach?"

"Yes?"

"Could we move the ball for my turn?"

The rest of the team groaned as Coach Davis shook his head. "It wouldn't be fair to move it closer, just for you."

Jeff straightened up, threw back his shoulders, and asked, "Closer? I don't want the ball closer."

"Then what?" his coach asked.

"I wanted to try from farther back."

Several of the players jeered.

"How far back?" the coach asked.

"Yeah, how far back?" Denny taunted. "The thirty?"

Jeff shook his head. "Put it on the thirty-five."

That caused an uproar from the whole team, but Coach Davis ordered the holder to take up his position.

Jeff limped over, carefully measured off his steps, then leaned forward. Three steps later he buried his big right foot into that ball. The pigskin rocketed off the ground, soared into the air, and cleared the goalposts with three feet to spare.

Every mouth on the team, including the manager's and coach's dropped open. A collective gasp followed.

"Can you do that again?" one of the players squealed.

Jeff took four more turns, and each kick was perfect.

"How did you ever learn to do that?" the coach asked.

Jeff looked toward the ground. "It was the last thing my dad taught me. I might be able to have an operation some day, but he said this foot was a special gift."

Finally, since Denny knew so much about kicking, Coach made him the holder. Jeff may not have been able to run fast. And it's true that he couldn't jump very high. But man . . . could that boy ever kick a football.

☆ *Peggy Duffy* ☆

Peggy Duffy grew up in Yonkers, New York, at a time when girls did not play sports. She buried herself in books instead and managed to survive childhood. Like her character Tina, she had lots of experience with parental embarrassment. Duffy is a first

generation American whose parents' first language is not English. This has led to a lifelong fascination and exploration through her writing of how people communicate in a language that is not their native one.

Duffy lives in Centreville, Virginia, with an extremely smart husband and an affectionate cat, who perches on her lap while she writes. She has an MFA in Creative Writing from George Mason University and has overcome her childhood inertia. She runs two miles a day. Her two daughters and son (now grown) finally taught her how to play soccer.

Song of Hope

by
Peggy Duffy

My mother, she doesn't understand at all.

I tell her, Coach says if we don't come to soccer practice, we don't get to play in the game on Sunday.

She says, "I need you come shopping with me." I nod my head and obey. It is Korean way. Come Sunday I sit on the bench, hanging my head, wanting more than anything to get my foot on the ball. The final score is one to one. Tie game. I know if the coach had put me out on the field, I would have helped score a goal.

After the game, Coach says, "Coming to practice tomorrow?"

"Yes," I say.

When I get home, I take off my cleats and leave them outside the door beside the new navy blue shoes I helped my mother buy last week. I told the man which ones she wanted to try on, what size she wore, which pair she finally decided to buy. I counted out the money and made sure she got the correct change.

"How was game?" my mother asks. She is at the kitchen sink draining salted water from chopped cabbage for kim chi.

"Okay. How was church?" I say.

She never comes to the games. Sunday is church day. I go to church in the morning, but my mother stays all day. Everyone in church speaks Korean. Sunday is why after three years in the United States my mother has never learned to speak English. No more than a few words. *Hello. Yes, please. Thank you very much.* She makes do by smiling and nodding her head like a bouncy ball, pretending she understands.

My mother, she doesn't understand at all.

I was in the sixth grade when we moved here for father's job. "You get to learn English," my grandmother said when she kissed me good-bye at the airport. "How lucky is that?"

Not lucky at all. I wasn't placed in a regular classroom. I was placed in a special class. No one else in the class spoke Korean. No one but the teacher spoke English. All day long we colored pictures. Pictures of houses. Pictures of family. Pictures of food. There were lines and loops printed beneath each picture.

"These are letters," the special teacher said. "These letters make words."

I didn't learn English in the special class. I didn't learn English from father who works long days and comes home too tired to speak even in Korean with me and mother.

I learned English from watching TV. I learned that my last name, Song, is American word for music. I like American music. More than anything, I wanted to know what their songs said. So every day after school I sat in front of the TV. One day it clicked what all those words meant. Americans sing of love. They sing of heartbreak. They sing of hope. They don't sing of obedience.

My teacher was so proud. She moved me into the regular class. My mother was so happy. She no longer needed to point to what she wanted at the store. She had me to talk.

At the sink my mother holds the cabbage under running water to rinse off the salt. She washes each piece three times. "Tomorrow I have errands to run," she says in Korean.

"Tomorrow I have soccer practice," I say in same language.

"Why always soccer practice?"

"Coach say," I tell her. I think she should understand such loyalty. But I forget. She gives me a look to help me remember. I am only child. I am also oldest daughter. Oldest daughter's responsibility is first to mother.

"Please, coach won't let me play if I don't go," I say.

"Is not so important, this game," she says. She tightens her lips and goes to work mixing green onions with garlic, chiles, ginger and water. Then she pours the mixture over the cabbage and stirs everything up in a big crock. A scowl is etched into her face, and her eyes disappear beneath tiny folds of skin. She thinks I should play the violin or the cello and be in the school orchestra. Or twirl around in a leotard in front of a wall of mirrors at dancing school and be in a recital on stage.

But I am a big girl, not little like she. I am stocky girl, thickset like grandfather way back in father's family. My fingers are too wide to press on one violin string without causing the one next to it to squawk like the geese we feed in the park, my feet too clumsy to stand long on toes for ballet. I topple over to one side. But I am a good soccer player. I run fast and have what Coach calls 'a big foot' that can kick the ball far up the field. He says I have a good chance of making the high school varsity team in a few years, but I need lots of play time with my club team. I want to tell this to my mother, but I don't know how to make her understand. I don't even know Korean word for varsity.

"There," my mother says, spooning the cabbage mixture into a large jar. "In a few days' time we have kim chi."

"In one day's time I have soccer practice."

"When?"

"Four o'clock."

She lowers a lid onto the jar. "Not done with errands by four o'clock."

I lower my eyes to the floor.

In English I say, "Thank you, thank you very much." I say it in a way that Americans call sarcastic, but I say it very soft, under my breath, so far under that I know the words will not rise to my mother's ears.

I do not want to disobey my mother, but if I don't go to practice today, there is no hope of me playing in the game and that would break my heart. So I do a very disobedient thing. When I leave for school the next day, I slip my cleats and shin guards into my backpack along with my books.

After school I go to the field and wait for everyone else to show up. Coach says, "Well Miss Song, I see you've finally decided to make a commitment to the team."

"Yes," I say. There's a note of that American sarcasm in his voice, but I pretend I don't hear it.

I practice hard. It is a hot day, the air sticky like fresh steamed rice. Sweat clings to my face. We practice drills for over an hour—foot skill drills, sprinting drills, give-and-go passing drills. Coach announces one last drill. I pass the ball, wipe the hot, salty sweat from my eyes and see my mother at the edge of the field, umbrella held high to keep the sun off her face. Even from this distance, I can't miss the scowl etched deep into the corners of her mouth. I run up the field to receive a pass, kick with the inside of my foot, but my timing is off. The ball boomerangs off my cleat and lands out of bounds.

Coach calls us off the field and divides us into two groups for a scrimmage. He nods his head toward where my mother stands. I don't look like my mother, but I am the only Korean girl on the team. It is easy for Coach to figure out whose mother she is.

Coach says, "She here to pick you up?"

"Yes," I say.

"Okay, fifteen more minutes and you can go."

But after the scrimmage, Coach decides we need to run. He tells us to do four laps around the field. I run hard as I can, pumping my legs so fast and hard they hurt, breathing even faster and harder until my lungs seem to gasp for air all on their own and my chest doesn't seem big enough to hold them. I run through all that pain. In a game it will be hot and tiring too, and I don't want to let my team down. I don't want to let my mother down either, but it is too late. I already have. I see the disappointment in her face each time I run past where she is standing behind the goal line.

When I finish the last lap, I see Coach walking toward my mother. I run over and beat him to her, still breathing hard, the sweat wet on my skin. My mother gives me a hard look, her lips held in a tight line, but then her face grows softer, eyes appearing again, as the Coach catches up to us.

Coach says, "So you're Tina's mom. It's good to meet you." He offers his hand.

My mother knows this American custom. She places her hand in his and shakes.

"Hello," she says, the big, toothy smile fixed on her mouth like it was painted on. I welcome a slight breeze, feel it dry the sweat on me, cooling my skin.

Coach says, "I'm glad to have Tina on my team. She's strong and fast and not afraid of the ball. And can she ever kick!"

My mother nods her head, teeth still showing. She is all white, like a soccer ball, with her pale skin the sun never shines on and her light teeth. "Thank you, thank you very much."

"Now we have to see about getting her to practice more," Coach says.

My mother nods again. The smile on her face stretches until the corners of her lips rise to the bottom of her ears, and her eyes look like two skinny caterpillars drawn in black crayon across the middle of her face. "Yes, please," she finally says.

Coach stands there for a long awkward silence. I know this silence.

"My mother doesn't understand," I say. He looks at me with his own frown of not understanding.

"She doesn't speak English," I add.

"Tell her I'm very glad to meet her and I think you are a good soccer player," he says, speaking very slowly and much too loud. I know this custom too. People always talk in this manner when they need me to translate. Like I can't hear if they don't raise their voices. Like I can't remember the words if they don't string them together with big empty spaces in between. I feel my face turn hot, even hotter than it felt running around the field.

My mother looks at me, waiting to hear what Coach has said. Very soft and fast, I tell her. My mother nods at Coach and says, "Thank you. Thank you very much." Her face is red and getting redder, but not from the sun. Not from the heat of running. Red like I have never seen on my mother's face.

Like she doesn't know anything just because she doesn't know English.

I turn and say something to her in Korean, not so softly this time. She says something back. Coach looks like he is waiting for me to translate again, but these words are only for my mother and me. I say something else to her and she smiles, but it is not painted-on smile.

What did I say? I said, "I'd like to see him try and speak Korean."

And she said, "It is not so easy to learn a language when you are old."

And I said, "You are not old. It just takes work and time, like to make kim chi. And you have me to teach you English. How lucky is that?"

Pretty lucky, from the smile on her face.

On the way to the car, she says, "Coach is not so nice. You really want to play soccer with him?"

"I love to play soccer," I say. "And this is the only chance I have to make the high school team one day."

She nods her head like maybe she understands. Then I think, this is America. Here you can fall in love and get your heart broken, but there is always hope. So I say, "Next week I have a game on Saturday."

She doesn't go to church on Saturday.

"Maybe," she says, "Maybe I come to game on Saturday.

"Thank you, thank you very much," I say, in that way Americans call sincere.